This Book Belongs To

FACES OF RAPMOTHERS

Book Two

Laurice Adams

Antonette Ames

Dianna Boss

Angela Guyton

Carlene Corsey

Tiffani Lewis

Rolanda Macharia

Candy Mitchell

Fedra Thompson

Jamika Wisdom

Sharon Young

CANDY STROTHER
DEVORE MITCHELL

FACES OF RAP MOTHERS

Beat Deep Books | *DonnaInk Publications, L.L.C.*

United States of America

CANDY STROTHER DEVORE MITCHELL

FACES OF RAP MOTHERS

by

CANDY STROTHER
DEVORE MITCHELL

CANDY STROTHER DEVORE MITCHELL

Beat Deep Books Imprint
An imprint of DonnaInk Publications, L.L.C.
17611 Aquasco Road
Brandywine, MD 20613

Library of Congress Cataloging-in-Publication.
Mitchell, Candy Strother DeVore, author. Quesinberry, Donna, Introduction and ghostwriter w/credit; Collins, Jeffrey, Foreword.
Title: Faces of Rap Mothers / Candy Strother DeVore Mitchell.
194 p. cm.

Subjects: BIO004000-BIOGRAPHY & AUTOBIOGRAPHY/Music; BIO032000 -BIOGRAPHY & AUTOBIOGRAPHY / Social Activists; BIO022000 BIOGRAPHY & AUTOBIOGRAPHY / Women; MUS031000-MUSIC / Genres & Styles / Rap & Hip Hop; MUSIC / Genres & Styles / Rhythm & Blues see Genres & Styles / Soul & R 'n B; SOC028000 SOCIAL SCIENCE / Women's Studies; SOC001000 SOCIAL SCIENCE / Ethnic Studies / African American Studies.

Identifiers: ISBN – 13 – 9781947704435, 9781947704930 or 9781947704848; ISBN – 13 – 9781947704626.

Printed in the United States of America

First Edition: 12 11 10 9 8 7 6 5 4 3 1 Edition; 2020. All Rights Reserved.

For more information contact:
DonnaInk Publications, L.L.C.: contact@donnainkpublications.com
www.donnaink.net | www.donnalquesinberry.com | www.facesofrapmothers.com

ACCOLADES

NOTES FROM
INDUSTRY AND REVIEWS

Soul Central Magazine's Mark Rowe nominated *Faces of Rap Mothers, Second Edition - Book One*:

"The Most Entertaining Hip-Hop Book in 2019."

Reviews:
Amazing book, amazing author! A must read!
Ms. Bonnie Williams – Late Stanley "Tookie" Williams Wife

". . . I love learning about the talent and new talent that has come out of the hip hop community. Everybody will love this book . . . reminds me of the Behind the Music . . . gives a glimpse of the portrayals and truths about hip hop . . .
Cheyenne – Rap Artist

OTHER BOOKS

BY CANDY STROTHER DEVORE MITCHELL

Rap Mothers Save The Day Series

Book One - 02/13/20

Book Two – 11/30/21

Book Three – 11/15/25

Book Four – TBA

Book Five – TBA

Book Six – TBA

Book Seven – TBA

Book Eight – TBA

Book Nine – TBA

Book Ten – TBA

Faces of Rap Mothers Book Series

Faces of Rap Mothers™ - Book One – 02/13/20

Faces of Rap Mothers™ - Book Two – 10/01/20

Faces of Rap Mothers™ - Book Three – 12/15/20

Faces of Rap Mothers™ - Book Four – 10/31/21

Faces of Rap Mothers™ - Book Five – TBA

Faces of Rap Mothers™ - Book Six – TBA

Faces of Rap Mothers™ - Book Seven – TBA

Faces of Rap Mothers™ - Book Eight – TBA

Faces of Rap Mothers™ - Book Nine – TBA

Faces of Rap Mothers™ - Book Ten – TBA

Faces of Rap Mothers®™© Fathers Editions

Book One – 11/25/21

Book Two – TBA

Book Three – TBA

Book Four – TBA

Book Five – TBA

Book Six – TBA

Book Eight – TBA

Book Nine – TBA

Book Ten – TBA

Faces of Rap Mothers®™© Presents . . .

Group X - Book One – 11/07/21
Curvy Queens of Dallas - Book Two – 03/07/22
Book Three – TBA
Book Four – TBA
Book Five – TBA
Book Six – TBA
Book Seven – TBA
Book Eight – TBA
Book Nine – TBA
Book Ten – TBA

HONORARIUM

JAMIE PARIS

DonnaInk Publications, L.L.C. | Beat Deep Books Copyright Protected

JAMIE JEANETTE PARIS
Funeral Service Scheduled
for Friday Oct. 18 @ 2pm

Angelus Funeral Home

3875 Crenshaw Blvd, Los Angeles Ca 90008
(323) 296 - 6666

SUNDAY MOOD

Family is Forever

"A beautiful woman delights the eye; a wise woman, the understanding; a pure one, the soul.
~ Minna Antrim

DAUGHTER
MOTHER
SISTER
FRIEND

DonnaInk Publications, L.L.C. | Beat Deep Books Copyright Protected

A MOTHER & HER SON

ORIGINAL RAP MOTHER

JAMIE PARIS

"I know for certain that we never lose the people we love, even to death. They continue to participate in every act, thought and decision we make. Their love leaves an indelible imprint in our memories." —Leo Buscaglia

Lights that Shine Eternal

A beautiful face can attract your heart
but a beautiful soul can connect with yours.

Jamie Paris

Soul Control Magazine Tribute

"The free soul is rare but you
know it when you see it -
basically because you feel good,
very good when you are near or
with them." - Charles Bukowski

DEDICATION

SHONTA RENEE GIBSON

Faces of Rap Mothers – Book Two, is dedicated to Shonta Renee Gibson, who is also known as "Queen G." Shonta is my best friend, and an amazing business associate. She loves sharing my titles and her assistance with marketing, next to my publisher, contributors, and assists, such as Mark Rowe of *Soul Central Magazine* from United Kingdom, has taken us to a new level of success. Many of my projects are enhanced by Queen G's industry knowledge and resources.

It's good to have associates willing to sacrifice time and energy to aid a friend's vision. Thank you, Queen G, for novel ideas and for inspiring all the Rap Mothers through your unwavering participation and assistance to see us succeed!

About Shonta Renee Gibson "Queen G":

Shonta Renee Gibson, better known in the rap and hip-hop community as, "Queen G" is a public figure best known for her work as a blogger, entertainment writer, and interviewer with a thriving career that has spanned twenty years in doing what this Queen loves.

In 2016, Queen G's life took a detour when she traveled to Las Vegas from LA, she was very tired having been up all-night doing hair for clients there. Shonta heard an inner voice, and believed God wanted her to get home quickly. Under fatigue, she followed her voice. When she arrived home, she walked to the door of their home and was happy to see her family who greeted her with open arms. As she began dinner preparation for the family, she noted it was about the equivalent of 113 degrees outside.

"Anyone who knows Vegas, knows the heat shares a distinction relative to hell," Shonta furthers, "My husband stepped outside to smoke in a pair of shorts and literally, he took one puff and immediately came back inside." She glimpsed at him as he plopped down in the lounge chair not having control over his body.

Shonta saw his face slump before her eyes. He tried to mouth the words, "I love you." His speech was slurred. It was as if he'd been to the dentist and was numbed. Holding him up in the chair, Shonta dialed 911. About seven minutes later, the ambulance arrived, but she remembers it felt like hours, "It was very scary."

When EMS looked at her husband, they identified he was having a serious stroke. The upcoming days proved challenging for the family due to the uncertainty of how long his recovery was going to take. It took some time, but he recovered; however, he could no longer work in the extreme heat and subsequently lost his job. It was then, the nightmare of homelessness began. Shortly after his release from the hospital - the family was evicted. For the first time, there wasn't a "solid plan" regarding where to go or what to do for the family. Shonta was in shock, but "still" as an entertainer she had the sense to know keeping their situation private would be her wisest decision.

With four children, their life was packed into the family vehicle. While the couple were able to stay with friends for a week or two – they didn't have money to work with and when her husband and the children's father could not work - it was not easy.

Shonta had to ask friends for help and she felt it was the most humbling experience she'd lived through. There were limited programs and resources for families in Vegas who were homeless at the time. Hotel vouchers took time to acquire. Asking for help from the County proved nearly impossible. Everything held a lengthy process. At times, the family was able to get a hotel room; other times they had to sleep in the car. When their income did kick in - they afforded a weekly stay at a kitchenette, which was a breath of fresh air. When money ran out and resources from folks they knew tapped out, Shonta, her husband and their children lived on a wing and a prayer with only God and their faith to keep them going. It felt like a nightmare had befell them that would not end.

Shonta felt like a tortured soul and did not have a solid answer for her children, which broke her heart. In spite of it all – she and her husband managed to keep the children in school who attended four different schools within a very short period of time due to moving around while homeless. It drained them all emotionally. Many mornings the couple washed their babies in the gas station bathrooms to prepare them for school. Then they combed their children's hair in the back seat of their truck.

Queen G's Inspirational Message:

"I wasn't going to allow my children to fail even though we felt like failures as parents. On one afternoon, walking through Molasky Park and thinking about our situation, I spotted a beautiful couple who were evidently also homeless. They appeared not to allow their circumstances to get to them; so, I stopped to speak with them. The entire time I was homeless, I still interviewed for entertainment programs. My natural instincts were always investigative.

"While talking to the couple and hearing their back story, a spiritual voice spoke to me stating, *Look around.* So, I glanced around the park and noted there were many homeless people. The voice of God spoke to me again, *This is your new mission. I want you to feed my people in this park.* At that moment, I was unaware of how I would feed people who weren't able to manage, when we couldn't manage for ourselves, but I knew not to go against the voice I heard.

"In the following month, while still living in a weekly, my husband and I listened to the prompting I'd received. We prepared spaghetti, rolls, salad, and banana pudding and bought bottled water. We wanted to share meals we would eat ourselves. The two of us said a prayer, took the food to the park, and served the homeless. The next month two volunteers joined us. The following month four volunteers joined, then fourteen, then forty-two – the vision grew by leaps and bounds.

"As we continued, we started filming and photographing our experiences and took them to social media. We filmed documentaries about homelessness under the tunnels of Las Vegas. What happened to us was incredibly sad and life changing, but I learned as we went through the process, we had compassion for the people we served.

"We named our mission *Operation Bring Your Best*. More volunteers joined. Eventually, we were giving homeless clothes, groceries, shoes, toiletries, etc. and the 'operation' became a huge success. The homeless began to depend on us. It touched my heart to see people get help through our mission. A DJ in Vegas named DJ Thump took notice of our mission and booked me as the first *Community Spotlight* guest on Power 88.

"His radio program aired mornings and prime time. DJ Remixx also showed us love on his Sunday radio mix as well. *Soul Central* and *On The Rise Magazine* spotlighted us too. In the months that followed I was awarded, *Sister of the Year* from Minister Stretch at a huge community festival.

"Through this mission I learned life belongs to a higher power and to follow the path of my inner voice, which is spirit. I grew to understand why our life changes and when it does, we must trust in the process, and trust in the Lord.

"Our homeless nightmare turned into a calling and I now believe; everything happens for a reason. Our homelessness lasted an entire year. Once we finally got into a new home, I had to pinch myself because I couldn't believe it was real. Our family passed life's test and arrived with a new life mission while keeping our family solid."

Children Are Inspiration

#QueenGLiveExperience

Laughter, the BEST Medicine!

From the moment I picked your book up until I laid it down, I was convulsed with laughter. Someday I intend reading it.
–Groucho Marx.

CANDY STROTHER DEVORE MITCHELL

TABLE OF CONTENTS
SHAPE OF THINGS TO COME

EPIGRAPH

TUPAC SHAKUR

'Life is a wheel of fortune and it's my turn to spin it'

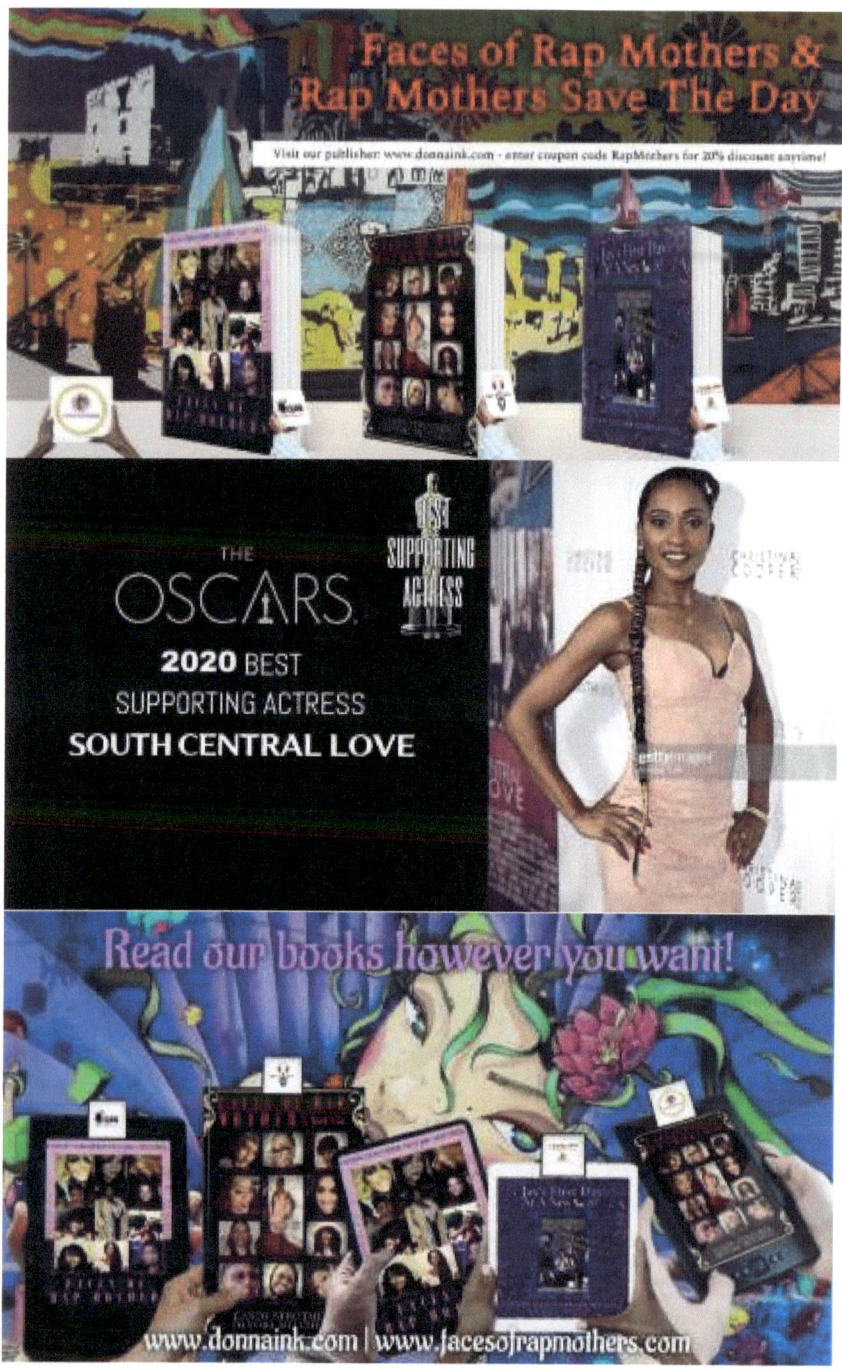

FOREWORD

JEFFREY COLLINS

A mother's work is never done.

Jeffrey Collins

Prior to Candice becoming a rap mother (i.e.: a woman with a son and daughter who like to rap and record songs), she was an advocate for civil rights. Her upbringing involved some of America's most revered civil and human rights activists, including her aunt Dr. Ophelia DeVore. Candy has been involved in entertainment and media since her early youth. Her extended family is entrenched in the entertainment industry, which doesn't mean Candy was handed industry recognition because she has had to earn props at every stage of her life.

Mitchell has become a rap and hip-hop mother for two of her children: HONEY and KING THA RAPPER. She had the good fortune, as a teen, to have extremely influential friends who are well-known rap and hip-hop artists. Again, this did not predispose her children. Instead, hard work to become educated in entertainment and media while accessing commercial programs at young ages, led the path to their current rap and hip-hop personas. Ultimately, resulting in the Faces of Rap Mothers book idea. Once Candy's children were hooked on music, she began talking with other mothers, sisters, aunts, cousins, and friends involved in the rap and hip-hop industry.

Candy's Rap Mothers programming began on YouTube with limited success. She identified the need for a book and publisher, which was achieved through acquaintance, Gilbert "Jalapeno" Jacobo and resulted in two book series: Faces of Rap Mothers and Rap Mothers Save the Day. The first, *Faces of Rap Mothers*, is a ten-volume series releasing up to 2030 by Beat Deep Books Imprint of **Donna**Ink Publications, L.L.C. The second, *Rap Mothers Save The Day*, is also a ten-volume series of children's books also releasing up to 2030 by Little Buggy Productions Imprint of **Donna**Ink Publications, L.L.C. *Book One* of *Faces of Rap Mothers*, was released in first- and second-edition and nominated *The Most Entertaining Hip-hop Book of 2019*!

Included in this, *Faces of Rap Mothers – Book Two*, an additional compilation of contributory stories from Rap Mothers with stories and images are included in this title. This new set of Rap Mothers are interesting rap and hip-hop lovers and all other readers. My sincere congratulations to Candice on this newest endeavor.

About Jeffrey Collins:

Mr. Collins heads Universal Digital Distribution. He is a senior business consultant for several major artists and entertainment companies including, Famous Music Group.

Having managed agencies, and booking well-known acts such as Dusty Springfield, Joe Cocker, Led Zeppelin, Lonnie Donegan, Moody Blues, The Beatles, etc. artisans Collins represented also included soul singer Donnie Elbert and Warren Davis Monday Band, etc., Jeffrey began a chain of retail record stores and a wholesale distribution company throughout the 70's and into the early 80's. He also produced recording artists, developing Echo Records and Vista Sounds. He created reggae albums with releases from Dennis Brown, Gregory Issacs, Johnny Clarke, etc. with over one hundred (100) additional famous artists. His vocation brought more internationally known artists and producers from Europe, Jamaica, and the United States. In 1983, he setup an independent recording studio in Englewood, New Jersey and achieved great successes.

From this base, JC successfully worked with Adina Howard, Boogie Down Productions / KRS-ONE, Brenda K. Starr, Chill Rob G., Colon-El Abrams, Father MC, G-DEP, GRAVE-DIGGAZ, Positive K., Ram Squad, Ready For The World, Sunz Of Man, Wu-Tang Clan, and a host of other artists that obtained "major label recording deals" with MCA, JIVE, KOCH, and others.

Although he could have retired at 50, when he moved with his family to Coral Springs, Florida, the call of music was still too loud to be ignored. He decided in 2004, to once more enjoy the challenges involved in the recording industry and determined to keep doing what he loves best.

After first setting up a warehouse filled with vinyl records, Jeffrey became a consultant for a record pressing and CD plant, based in Plantation, Florida. He then started a new digital record label, Famous Records, Corporation, which releases and promotes music for artists worldwide via Universal Digital Distribution.

FAMOUS RECORDS / UNIVERSAL DIGITAL
Tel: 954-366-7419
Cell: 954-817-2878
Skype: jeffrey.echovista
www.UniversalDigitalDistribution.com

PREFACE

STORY OF
FACES OF RAP MOTHERS

Candy Strother DeVore Mitchell is a lifelong innovator. Raised in a family steeped among public figures in both entertainment and political landscapes, Mitchell's Rap Mothers venture is a natural result. When reading, *Faces of Rap Mothers – Book One* the history of Mitchell's upbringing amazes readers. From Ophelia DeVore (America's first African American recognized model and modeling agency owner), to incorporation of R&B's leading performance artists who are fathers, stepfathers, uncles, cousins conjoined by equally impressive sisters, stepsisters, aunts, and nieces . . . ; it becomes apparent "not" being in entertainment or "music arts" would mean not being a member of the family – at least that is readers' take-away. Let's just say, Mitchell's lifetime media engagement was predetermined at birth. And, with her natural ability to gain others' interest, Candy is relentless and doesn't take "no" for an answer.

As an individual, Mitchell is an engaging woman – who says want you want to hear with a refreshing grace. Her ideas springboard others. If Mitchell has a foible, it is how her ideas are used to fuel lives while hoping they all combine in unified vision.

How a book comes to be in existence is often as interesting as the book, itself!

You may wonder, how an author's idea becomes a book, and how a book becomes nominated as "The Best Hip-hop Book of 2019" with a follow-on nationally televised program?

Well . . . great questions deserve truthful answers!

Luckily, for readers, Mitchell is an author who believes sharing is wealth! *Faces of Rap Mothers* and *Rap Mothers Save The Day* share developmental stories, which "may" benefit readers envisioning unique projects themselves.

Originally, Mitchell had the YouTube program, *The Faces of Rap Mothers* with limited participation as stated earlier; however, her concept, though budding, was well-received communally among rap and hip-hop artists . . . before a good book . . . is a good concept.

Being the smart woman Mitchell is, she stepped up to the plate as opportunities arose to move her budding idea to a realized dream. Mitchell knew a book would move her work forward. When her friend, Gilbert "Jalapeno" Jacobo stated he was developing a book and having have his personal story ghostwritten, Mitchell inquired if she could engage his ghostwriter. At the time, Mr. Steven Kay, ghostwriter, and author, had been working with Jacobo. Kay, from United Kingdom, had been flown to Los Angeles by Jacobo to work with him on his book. While Kay worked with Jacobo – he joined in a visit to Mitchell's home with Jacobo who introduced the two. At the time, Mitchell connected with Kay on social media and asked for his assistance with her autobiography book idea. Kay agreed and, Jacobo accepted their arrangement.

Jacobo met with industry reps showing interest in moving his story into a script and follow-on movie. This was also of interest to Mitchell. Kay created Jacobo's manuscript, which Jacobo felt didn't align 100% to concepts he wanted projected within the context. Kay determined to return to the United Kingdom shortly thereafter.

Jacobo, principal of a 501(c)3, Affiliated People's Alliance (APA), includes Mitchell on the Board of Directors. APA is a Family Court and Human Rights Reform Advocacy. Jacobo being friends with Ms. Donna L. Quesinberry's (Mitchell's ghostwriter and publisher) daughter, Ms. Danielle Hatcher, also a Family Court Reform Advocate learned about **Donna**Ink through Hatcher. Jacobo and Hatcher knew one another through industry affiliations and during general conversation, discussed his book. Hatcher shared her mother, Quesinberry (known as "Q" by her friends), publishes and ghostwrites books. Later, while Jacobo was on the telephone with Hatcher, Q stopped in to visit her daughter, who put Jacobo and Q on the phone together. After discussion about ghostwriting and publishing,

Jacobo asked Q to look at his manuscript and consider finalizing and publishing it.

Q agreed to consider it. Afterward, Q forwarded title representation materials for Jacobo's information. And discussions with Kay began not long afterward, in discussing elements of ghostwriting he had completed for Jacobo, which resulted in Kay's request to be published in America through Q's **DonnaInk Publications, L.L.C.**

Shortly thereafter, Jacobo and Hatcher began working more closely as advocates. Jacobo planned a trip from LA to North Carolina where Hatcher resides to work on Family Court and Human Rights Reform and Hatcher was also invited on APA's Board of Directors. When visiting Hatcher, Jacobo met Q.

After meeting, Jacobo and Q held more meetings discussing development of his book. APA was working on an impending Human and Children Rights Movement event at an LA college where Mitchell was spearheading participation alongside Bonnie Williams (e.g.: Stanley Tookie Williams wife) and their son Trayvon – both human rights activists involved in redressing the former Tookie Williams community impact. As Jacobo and Mitchell discussed the impending event on mobile, Mitchell and Q were put on the phone and introduced.

In the interim, Kay prepared for return flight to the United Kingdom. He reviewed and then signed title representation agreement with Q for his nearly ten novels through **DonnaInk Publications, L.L.C.** Ironmantle Press (e.g.: romance) shelf. Since Kay's engagement with Jacobo ended and he was headed back to the UK – no conflict of interest (COI) existed. Q agreed it was okay to accept Kay's works. Before his departure, Kay worked on Mitchell's book as ghostwriter of her autobiographical fiction title – originally more autobiography in nature. Due to this, Kay is credited in *Faces of Rap Mothers* series releases as an originating ghostwriter. Q and Mitchell agree on appropriately recognizing people involved in creative processes, especially originators.

Both Mitchell and Q, during their call with Jacobo, shared social media information and began dialoguing fall of 2018. Mitchell immediately requested Q's assistance as a ghostwriter and publisher during the impending year. Originally, Q refused because Jacobo's title was ongoing and a COI could exist.

With Jacobo a friend of Hatcher's, Q believed familial relationships trump budding entrepreneurial projects – no matter who the parties are. As time moved forward, Jacobo and Q held creative differences regarding their work and Jacobo subsequently found a new ghostwriter. Mitchell continued prompting Q who finally agreed to ghostwrite and publish her books through **Donna**Ink **Publications, L.L.C.** Beat Deep Books; and for *Rap Mothers Save the Day,* the Little Buggy Productions Imprint (e.g.: children's).

Faces of Rap Mothers, originally presented as a standalone title, after 2nd Re-editioned release when Mark Rowe, CEO of *Soul Central Magazine* nominating the title as "The Most Entertaining Hip-Hop Book of 2019" converted to a ten-book series for the five-year (extended another five years) title representation agreement Mitchell engaged Q and **Donna**Ink **Publications, L.L.C**.

As with all new book releases . . . nearly two-thirds of the contributors, friends and associates of Mitchell contacted Q to request stories be ghostwritten and published for them too. One such request came from Shonta Renee Gibson, Tyrese Gibson's sister, known as Queen G and showed promise; however, **Donna**Ink has not signed any additional Rap Mothers since signing Mitchell.

Queen G, Shonta Gibson, being totally immersed in Mitchell's Rap Mothers project has been so helpful she was chosen for Mitchell's Dedication of *Book Two*. After Queen G approached Q who has an ironclad rule not to publish "any" author family or friends within first year of a new release, especially as a novice author. And, this did not slow Queen G down, who has gone on to develop her own books. Q's rule ensures authors maintain limelight the first year of publication within their inner circle. It is Q's experience that things get murky otherwise and an author's work can be unfairly diminished. As well, a good book idea normally comes from an author, not after seeing an author's success.

Queen G has published approximately five children's books and eight biographical and/or self-help shorts concerning entertainment and self-help all within less than one year. What an amazing feat! With only a few feature co-authors, her accomplishments really garner the attention of fellow Rap Mothers.

Mitchell suggested Q may not want to publish some Rap Mothers' works but Q reiterated publishing house policy is not to mix abundance with too many parties in the same sphere due to OCI and other issues. Until an originating author is off the ground and running – it is proven to be unpleasant business to begin publishing their friends and loved ones. For instance, Q still feels poorly Jacobo's book is in development while his requires specifications in content that are not easily produced and by their nature take longer – it remains saddening to Q. Since, Jacobo introduced Mitchell to **DonnaInk** and got her works' rolling it is disheartening Jacobo's title didn't release first. Out of respect and recognition, Jacobo receives credit each release of *Faces of Rap Mothers* and shout outs are appropriate to Hatcher and Kay for their introductions as well. Mitchell's book may never have been introduced to rap and hip-hop community as Rowe's "Most Entertaining Hip-Hop Book of 2019" with quality results. Queen G said it best,

> *"You really opened my eyes – I've never thought about writing a book – this is great. I don't know why I didn't think of this before. This really has me motivated. I'm excited!"*

So a big vote of thanks goes to Jacobo, Hatcher, Kay, Q, author Candy Strother DeVore Mitchell as well as contributing Rap Mothers:

Laurice Adams, Antonette Ames, Honey Blunt, Dianna Boss,
Jeffrey Collins, Carlene Corsey, Shirley Curley, Duv Mac

Dg, Shonta Gibson, Angela Gilchrist-Guyton, Tyaunna Harris, Angel Hicks, Rolanda Shemwell Greer Macharia, Lena Moss, Jamie Paris, Jamika Smith, Fedra Thompson, Nina Womack, and Sharon Lynette Young.

Once the release of *Faces of Rap Mothers* in *Book One* and the *Re-editioned Book One (2ⁿᵈ Edition)* . . . Rap Mothers really got behind Mitchell's project. New doors continue to open for each of these women. At this time, Rap Mothers through Mitchell, and Queen G feature a program nationally, on the NOW Network. Their efforts are moving toward reality television and through their associations may really kick-off!

So . . . in answer to the question: *how an author's idea becomes a book a nominated as "The Best Hip-hop Book of 2019" with a follow-on nationally televised program?* The answer in part is through association but this can be created with effort. So, the follow-on answer is not giving up and relentlessly pursue your desired outcome.

If Mitchell had dropped off the vine when her initial request to be published resulted in, "No, I think it would be inappropriate under the circumstances": the NOW Network program wouldn't prevail in the current hour. A good idea becomes a tangible result through dedication, desire, intention, and the stickability factor™. So . . . there you have it! Until next Book Three release . . . remain dedicated to your ideas and don't take "no" for an answer! More in "Book Three!"

CANDY STROTHER DEVORE MITCHELL

Author & Ghostwriter Steven Kay

**A DONNAINK PUBLICATIONS ROMANCE AUTHOR
IRONMANTLE BOOKS IMPRINT**

STEVEN KAY TITLES

FOR THE LOVE OF MY CHILDREN
IN WORDSWORTH'S SHADOW
PEBBLES: LOVE ACROSS THE MORECAMBE BAY
THE SATANIC COURT
THE VICAR OF BUTTERMORE
YOU AND ME
WORDSWORTH'S BABY

DonnaInk Publications, L.L.C. extends special thanks to Robert Jacobs and Candy Strother DeVore Mitchell for introducing Mr. Steven Kay and his works.

ACKNOWLEDGEMENTS

CANDY STROTHER
DEVORE MITCHELL

DonnaInk Publications, L.L.C. | Beat Deep Books Copyright Protected
xlviii

At this time, I want to take a moment to acknowledge everyone who helped bring this book forward. First, I thank God for his direction moving me toward an abundant outlook in life. He aids me in all things I set out to achieve and has delivered triumphs in my professional and home life.

My family and friends have aided with ideas in the development of my two series titles. Support and love from people included in my inner and outer circle I am indebted toward, for the love and support they deliver. My husband is my rock. Without my children and his support, this work would not be accomplished.

My contributors are kind to share stories and imagery. Their personal rap and hip-hop journeys are genuinely interesting. We share oneness in our love and respect for entertainment icons we've grown accustomed to. Moving through life, has been, and remains, an all-encompassing experience among rap and hip-hop's finest. Strong synergies we maintain with family and friendships are vital because they carry us through ups and downs associated with fame and its effects. As "Queens" living day-to-day, Rap Mothers reflect on our loved ones and their passions and how those attune to ours, which is a blessing.

An important honorable mention is directed toward Mr. Jeffrey Collins who wrote the Foreword to *Faces of Rap Mothers.* He is a world-renown director, producer, publicist, record label owner, and sound engineer who still serves up his over forty (40) plus years of expertise. Thank you, Mr. Collins, for taking your time to Foreword *Faces of Rap Mothers* series and "me" Candice. You are appreciated!

Also, a shout out to my publisher, **DonnaInk Publications, L.L.C.**, Beat Deep Books, and Little Buggy Productions, their imprints. A small, woman-owned, traditional publishing house, **DonnaInk** features more than thirty (30) eclectic authors and titles for discriminating readers. Q is my professional ghostwriter with credit and **DonnaInk Publications, L.L.C.** employs **dpInk Ltd. Liability Company** who create *Faces of Rap Mothers* and Rap Mothers Save The Day media and merchandise. For book and/or merchandise bulk orders write contat@donnainkpublications.com to have them hook you up!

Shout outs for Book Two go out to Ms. Danielle Hatcher, Mr. Gilbert "Jalapeno" Jacobo, and Mr. Steven Kay for introductions aiding publisher acquisition as parties in the first part. Most importantly, sincere thank you to readers, fans, and enthusiasts who are the ultimate reason for these books – thank you! Continue supporting rap and hip-hop artists and community platforms and enjoy these stories about their real-life personalities.

I pray each of you ENJOY this book and many more to come in the *Faces of Rap Mothers* and *Rap Mothers Save the Day* series!

PROLOGUE

BEGINNING
AND ENDING

Special Tribute To
Candy Strother DeVore Mitchell's
Mother

For starters, in *Faces of Rap Mothers – Book Two*, some chapters feature more background development than others – contributors determine what is provided to the author. Many chapters are photographic renderings where image and visual discernment is the contributor's desired takeaway for readers. Like all art, photographs are open to the observer discernment. Some images are old and worn and not industry images by professional photographers at red carpet events. Others are just that. Many images are from family events with friends or extended family and/or at friends' homes.

Let's face it . . . back in the day . . . photos were often taken using disposable cameras and developed at department stores or were infamous polaroid images for instant viewing. The cool aspect of these is homespun memories otherwise undisclosed to media.

Due to the reality of reproduction and/or regeneration of worn or tattered images through a modern lens being not as easy as one might suspect . . . please don't be judgmental. It is my hope, *Faces of Rap Mothers* permits readers a glimpse of enjoyments of life with extended family and friends, many who hail among the rich and famous of the rap and hip-hop industry.

For *Book Two*, the divider fleuron is an image of a rapper . . . when you see this . . . if you are not aware why it is included . . . this is where a natural pause occurs in a book. The image is a Creative Commons happy to glad addition to the title.

To purchase *Book Two* of *Faces of Rap Mothers* be aware the title is available in color soft cover or black and white (b/w). The titles are also available in hardcover color or black and white (b/w). An e-Edition may become available of *Book One* soon, followed by *Book Two* in e-Edition; additionally, an online electronic flip book is soon to be releasing. Signature copies can be made available upon request. Any / all signed copies will ship with unique timelines because signatures of all contributors from different cities and states take time to acquire.

Where able, names throughout my books are listed alpha-betically by last name or by group name when a last name isn't identified. This eliminates *Who's Who* in listing issues.

Okay, *this is meant* to entertain and educate regarding American folklore involved in rap and hip-hop. *Book Two* has arrived! Look for *Book Three* spring of 2021!

INTRODUCTION

MS. DONNA L. QUESINBERY

Faces of Rap Mothers originally presented as an independent title was added to *Rap Mothers Save The Day* children's books resulting in two ten-book series titles – ten for adult trades and ten for children. Once introduced to the rap and hip-hop community, "Book One," currently in 2nd Edition format, received nomination as "The Best Hip-Hop Book of 2019" from Mark Rowe of *Soul Central Magazine*! It became obvious a series of Rap Mother books was sensible. Working with **DonnaInk Publications, L.L.C.**, the decision to release "chapbooks" (e.g.: smaller shorts) quarterly, including "**new** rap and hip-hop ladies" each release; however, Mitchell's acquisition of stories with images being more intense and compilation of the books, coupled with the advent of Corona Virus (e.g.: COVID-19) resulted in a more logistical bi-annual production schedule to ensure quality publications for the rap and hip-hop community. Each year two books from *Faces of Rap Mothers* and *Rap Mothers Save The Day* release bi-annually for the next four to five years. This permits our author to schedule events, signings, and community interest engagements and to navigate new televised reality TV shows presently as subscribers, soon to be picked up for standard reception!

Faces of Rap Mothers – Book Two, includes the newest Rap Mothers who share stories with images and includes (e.g.: listed here alphabetically by last name):

1. Author Candy Strother DeVore Mitchell
2. Laurice Adams
3. Antonette Ames
4. Dianna Boss
5. Carlene Corsey
6. Angela Gilchrist-Guyton
7. Tiffani Lewis
8. Rolanda Shemwell Macharia
9. Fedra Thompson
10. Jamika Love Wisdom
11. Sharon Lynette-Young

It is my hope, as readers, you find Candy's newest book to be interesting and entertaining. Enjoy your copy of *Faces of Rap Mothers – Book Two*!

FACES OF
RAP MOTHERS

CANDY STROTHER DEVORE MITCHELL

CHAPTER ONE

CANDY STROTHER
DEVORE MITCHELL

Hey you all . . . I'm back at it again with *Faces of Rap Mothers – Book Two*. Our real stories are ongoing and share more entertaining facts of Hollywood happenings in the rap and hip-hop industry. Since my last title release (re-edition of *Book One* in February of 2020), contributors as Rap Mothers have been in many entertainment magazines worldwide. This includes a burgeoning group of publications from Mark Rowe: *Soul Central Magazine* in the United Kingdom and *The Last Hope of Untouchable Magazine* in the United States. I want to thank Mark for his love and support of *Faces of Rap Mothers – Book One* and now, *Book Two* as well as for *Rap Mothers Save The Day* children's books. Thank you, Mark for your undying support!!!!

The first half of 2020 has been full of ups and downs. Life in general has been fluid; however, we experienced a devastating event, which shocked the entire Rap Mother community. *Faces of Rap Mothers Book One* Contributor, Jamie Paris, suddenly died. All Rap Mothers are heartbroken, Jamie's passing was devastating. Rap Mothers Baretta, O.G. Lil Mama, West Coast Hip Hop Artist Honey and I supported Rap Sister Jamie Paris by attending her funeral and paying our respects to Queen Jamie in celebration of her amazing life.

Jamie is a Rap Mother I have known since age fourteen. She is rap artisan JP Cali Smoov's mom and we have agreed as Rap Mothers to continue to support him in his lifetime. All of us will continue to have a void in our day-to-day life without Jamie here in this earthly realm, but we continue to view Jamie as our Queen Angel of the *Faces of Rap Mothers* and *Rap Mothers Save The Day*.

My son, KING THA RAPPER has continued to remain involved in writing and performing as a *Black Cash Records*

artist. King is also producing my nephew as an up and coming mid-west Hip Hop artist, LKapone. He is from Gary Indiana. His works feature some really tight and beautiful music with some hot tracks being released soon.

My daughter, HONEY continued writing and recording new music daily. HONEY is learning to engineer, and I have to admit she is surprisingly good at it.

My son, Lawrence completed two years of service for the United States Army in January of this year. I keep him in prayer as always.

My son, Tyler Lee, and his soccer team have been training for championships. I gifted a copy of *Faces of Rap Mothers – Book One* to the team, which felt good and got to attend his games, which felt better!

In review of 2019, and the first half of 2020, the roller-coaster aspect of life has been a lot to endure. We've gotten through the Corona Virus (COVID-19) and deaths of influential African Americans from both accidents and at the hands of police officers, resulting in protests and rioting. These events and politics have consumed 2020 so far. I promised myself not to get political in my books and I'm holding myself to this promise - I must say though - so much has happened, which is sad and disheartening. I have to admit a strong belief in God is essential to keeping oneself in a good mental place in today's world.

Faces of Rap Mothers – Book One, in first release and the 2nd Edition of *Book One* were both accomplished by February 2020. And, a nomination was scored from *Soul Central Magazine* of my book as "The Best Hip-Hop Entertainment Book of 2019," which is an honor.

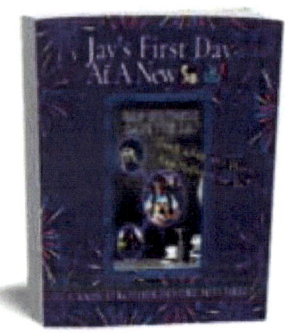 Also, *Rap Mothers Save The Day – Book One*, released in February 2020 both the re-edition and first "Rap Mothers Save The Day" series title published on the 13th of February – just in time for Valentine's Day. A nice gift from my publisher.

As I stated above, 2019 to 2020 has proven to be a full year with so many unusual developments including losses and winnings . . . I've had the ability to begin working with an amazing new talent, "Roxie" who is a super model, with many years of professional modeling experience. She is also a talented vocalist. Roxie has Whitney Houston lungs. I have to admit it feels pretty solid to watch her career grow; so . . . look for more about Roxie in *Book Three*.

A major honor in *Faces of Rap Mothers – Book Two*, is sharing actress Carlene Corsey, who was nominated for an Oscar in the production, "South Central Love" directed by Christina Cooper executive producer of Christina Cooper Productions. The movie shares the story of the unforgiving streets of Los Angeles, where we meet Bria and Davonte who are from two different worlds. Through trials and tribulations, they face, the couple realize how much they have in common - from broken families to friendships – growing closer, understanding how to impact change in their lives and community. Davonte learns to trust his intuition, make better decisions, and to break stereotypes of young African American males. Cooper created this film to encourage love within our city streets and put an end to gang violence. Of course, all Rap Mother stories revealed in *Book Two* are a treasure. It is my sincere hope you enjoy their stories and images as well. This, the second book of my ten-book series, is certain to become a collector set in the future. It is my belief readers will do to obtain all releases as collector's items. And, *Faces of Rap Mothers – Book Three* as well as *Rap Mothers Save The Day – Book Three* will be releasing spring of 2021! Take an opportunity to visit "The Faces of Rap Mothers" on the NOW Network and we'll begin our new reality television series together!

Celebrate Life, Love, Essence

Don't let bad days keep you down. Keep a childlike spring in your

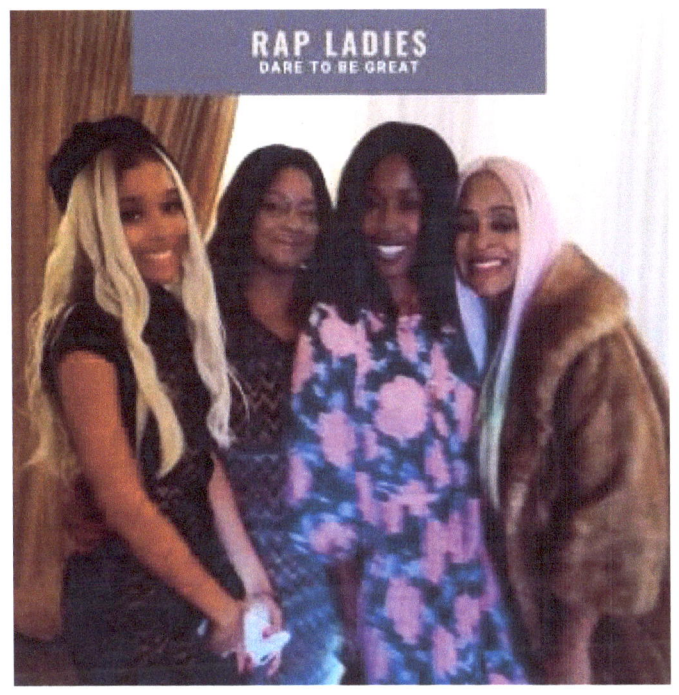

KING THA RAPPER

CHAPTER TWO

LAURICE ADAMS

LAURICE ADAMS-SIMMONS

Be beautiful, be stylish, and love yourself.

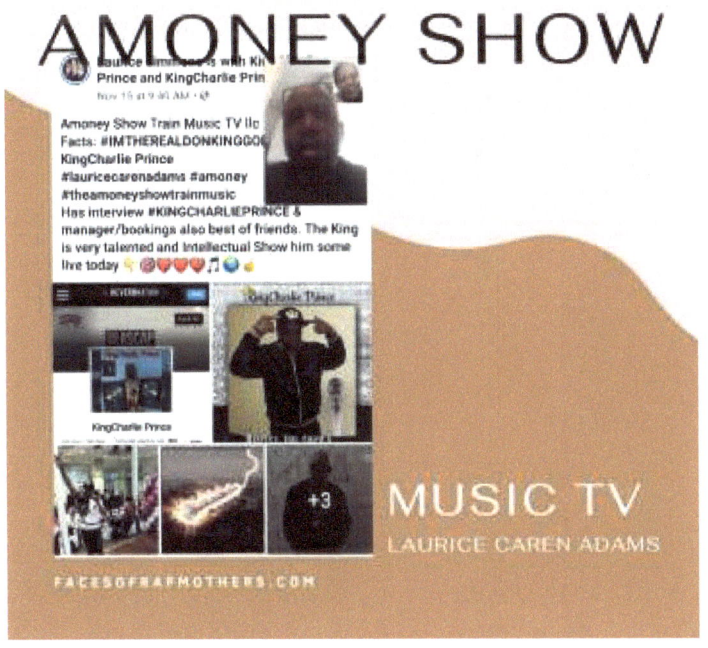

EACH DAY IS THE START OF SOMETHING NEW.

Choose your next adventure

www.facesofrapmothers.com

today is a good day for a good day

CANDY STROTHER DEVORE MITCHELL

WWW.FACESOFRAPMOTHERS.COM

Favored friends to shine with!

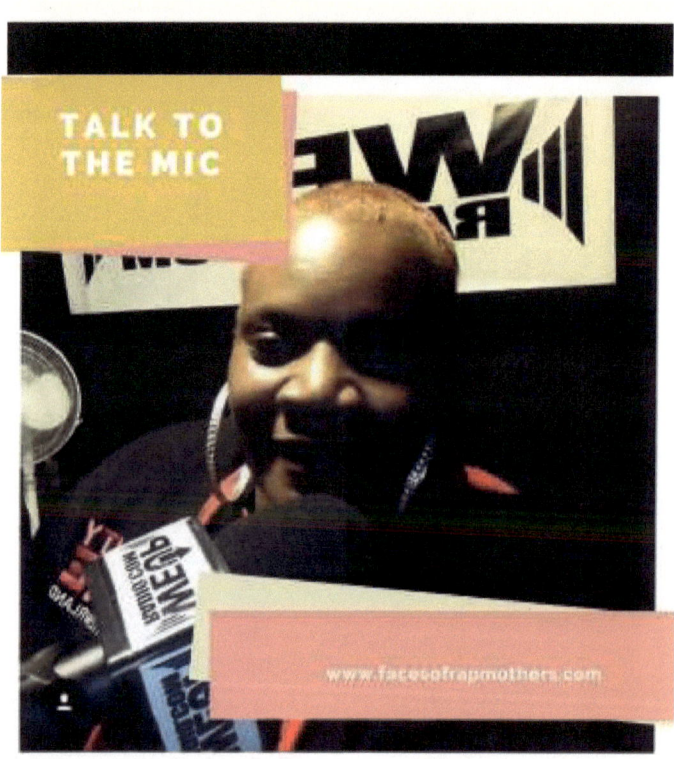

CHAPTER THREE

ANTONETTE AMES

About Antonette Ames, Founder & CEO of A H P

As Founder and CEO of Ames High Productions (A H P), Antonette Ames is also the niece of the legendary, late, Sylvester Ames, Jr., President of A&S Productions. Sylvester, Antonette's father, worked with Reverand Marvin Yancy, ex-husband of Natalie Cole (i.e.: daughter of the late Nat King Cole). Sylvester, Marvin, and Kevin Yancy formed MKS Productions. Sylvester produced a number of projects and albums – one of his contributions to industry is Fountain of Life Joy Choir with one of the songs lead by Natalie Cole and nominated for a Stellar Award in 1984-85.

Antonette's mother sang with the gospel group, "The Bernard Sisters." They sang across Chicago with legendary R&B group, "The Emotions," known in their early years as, "The Hutchinson Sunbeams." She also worked with major entertainment artists including, Rappin 4Tay, Mystical, Project Pat, Evan Lionel and Gerald Kelly.

It was inevitable Antonette would follow in the footsteps of these great men and women who preceded her within the music industry. Antonette began taking the music industry more seriously in 2004, where she planned Church events. She later planned her own major professional events in 2012 and beyond. Starting with a non-profanity gospel comedy show starring comedian Lester Barrie (i.e.: Def Comedy Jam all-star, Apollo Theater legend, and BET Comicview Host); Antonette managed two shows with Lester, an old grammar school classmate of hers from Chicagor Illinois. She later held an event with Grammy Award winner Le'Andria Johnson in 2015.

Today, Antonette continues in the industry through A H P and shares in *Faces of Rap Mothers* reality programming, books, magazines and additional ventures.

DA Smart

DA Smart was raised in both the Altgeld Murray and Robert Taylor projects. He is now the CEO and a living legend in Chicago-land area, ready to expand. His exploits are well-documented in Chicago.

When DA dropped the Chicago Anthem, "Walk Wit Me" the song was quickly acclaimed as one of the greatest songs ever made in Chicago hip-hop history. DA Smart has been blessed with the ability to move crowds with his magnetic personality, dynamic energetic stage presence, and entertaining, fun loving, hip-hop talent that spans over two decades. A leader and positive influence within his community, DA Smart has a passion to represent those who are lost, "hungry, naked, and outdoors."

DA's additional amazing talents as a battle and freestyle rapper have lead him to negotiations with big conglomerates like Columbia Records, Warner Bros. Records, Motown Records, and Jive Records. He signed to RCA Records and later to Creators Way Associated Labels, which carried Twista and Do Or Die. He holds many mile-stones that have enhanced his career and has sold over 10,000 copies in one day at the Million Man March in 1995 with his single "One In A Million."

DA Smart performed in the video, "Where Ya At," with IceT, Rza, Ice Cube, Chuck D, and Killah Priest. He even graced the great Eddie Kendricks video "Get it While it's Hot." Little known is his prestigious appearances with a star-studded lineup that includes KRS-One, Poor Righteous Teachers, Prince Markie Dee, A Lighter Shade of Brown, Cypress Hill, Public Enemy, and Twista. He toured Illinois prisons with Mc Lyte and was the first rapper to win the Regal Talent Show competition which jettisoned his already burgeoning career.

Now an independent artist, DA is Chief Executive Officer of the talented Terror Records label. His branding is continuing the household name built for himself and enhanced through the assistance of team of talents. DA Smart is part of the Legends of Hip-Hop, an organization acknowledging contributions of Illinois' Hip-Hop history movers and shakers.

Getting to the Core of the Female Rap Game: The Qor

The rap game is challenging. The industry is huge, there are many artists, producers, managers, and record labels to choose from. Some just care about lyrics while others care about beat. There are artists in it for the money and fame while others are in it to reach those who are lost. The rat race to get to Number One has been going on for ages and stars come and go.

The real question is who is next?

Born and raised in Chicago; later relocating to Denver Colorado, Kerisha Crowder was witness to the joys and losses of life. She was born into a strict household where she was encouraged to dream big but work hard. With both her parents in the music industry, she was exposed to music at an early age. Music, you can say, runs in her DNA. Her mother put together several sold out concerts and events and her father had extensive equipment with his lifelong passion for music. Her great-uncle has ties to the great Natalie Cole. The Qor was destined for greatness. At the age of 9, Kerisha broke down a karaoke machine she spilled juice on and put it back together effortlessly before her mother noticed. By the time she was 13 years old, she was writing her own creative pieces. At the age of 19, she began rapping and making beats using the music program Sonar.

As a woman rapper it's twice as hard. Female rappers have to sell records without selling their soul. Of course, the industry is filled with sex and grandeur. Breaking into the rap game is more than just having talent. "It takes grit, hard work, and money," CEO of Ames Production explains.

"I had to study The Qor's craft and speak with DJ's and help her with getting noticed." After a few shows and hits, The Qor finally got her break. She toured with afon.com and rocked the mic all across the United States. She was blessed with many gifts: sound engineering, video editor, photography, song writing and spitting hot 16s - just to name some of the skills she boasts. She considers herself a trendsetter and has worked with several heavy hitters in the music industry. Antonette Ames, of Ames Productions remembers The Qor's humble beginnings.

"I recall her working out of the closet in her apartment and her photos in front of her shower curtains.

I see the growth."

The debut album she created titled, "I Gotta Have It," has been released. It's available for download and online streaming from all major streaming services like Google Play, iTunes, Soundcloud, Spotify, etc. She's currently preparing to head back on tour with Ames Productions in a six-city tour. With more projects in the works, you can bet your last dollar, The Qor will be a household name very soon.

With great lyrics, attention to detail, and down-to-earth personality it's her time to shine!

RAP MOTHER

""It ain't no fun if the homies can't have none."

Snoop Dogg

"Few rappers realize the genre sprang from West African griots through Delta slave songs to jazz poetry and the comedic trash talk of 'the dozens.'" – Quincy Jones

AMES HIGH PRODUCTIONS

FACES OF RAP MOTHERS
WWW.FACESOFRAPMOTHERS.COM

RAP MOTHER

ANTONETTE AMES

WWW.FACESOFRAPMOTHERS.COM

CHAPTER FOUR

DIANNA BOSS

DIANNA BOSS

Dianna Boss grew up in South Central Los Angeles as the "only" girl among four children. She was the baby. Dianna met me thirty years ago. Her brother, T Bone Reed, was a member of the ROBOT BOYS who danced on *Soul Train*. He introduced Dianna and I.

T Bone danced with Chaka Khan, Snoop Dogg, and William Iam. T Bone lived in the same apartent complex in Hollywood as me, and due to this, I had the opportunity to grow a strong bond with her while we were young when she visited her brother.

Dianna Boss really made my day agreeing to become a Rap Mother for the *Faces of Rap Mothers* series books, agreeing to also participate in Rap Mothers add-on projects, including nationally and internationally televised programs. Dianna has agreed to serve as our "President of Marketing and Media!" Thank you Dianna!

An advocate for foster children regarding adoption, Dianna is also a foster parent who has successfully adopted children. She appreciates community work and outreach and looks forward to ignite more philanthropic work as a Rap Mother through uplifting and empowering people of every color, creed, and nationality.

I am blessed to have Dianna Boss as one of our Rap Mothers!

SPECIAL DAYS WITH SPECIAL PEOPLE

SPECIAL
DAYS
WITH
SPECIAL
PEOPLE

#FACESOFRAPMOTHERS

FAMILY
LOVE

WWW.FACESOFRAPMOTHERS.COM

WWW.FACESOFRAPMOTHERS.COM

TODAY IS A GOOD DAY
FOR A GOOD DAY.

CHAPTER FIVE

CARLENE
CORSEY

CARLENE CORSEY
Actress / Host

Height:5'2 Weight:105
Eyes:Brown Hair:Brown

ADDRESS
Los Angeles, CA

PHONE
213 590 8845

EMAIL
carlenecorseypr
@gmail.com

CREDITS

2019
KINGS SOLE (EXECT. PRODUCER &
LINE PRODUCER)

2019
SOUTH CENTRAL LOVE (MAMA DEE)

2019
CYCLES IN LOVE SHORT (AMANDA)

2018
LOYALTY SHORT (MAMA DEE)

2017
AVENGE THE CROWS (GANGSTA GIRL)

2013
AMERICA'S COURT
JUDGE ROSS (YVONNE MARTIN)

SPECIAL SKILLS

I am a born natural when it comes to
Acting I've been told and I have shown
it as well. I am easy to work with and
a great listener. I catch on quick and
also can assist to help any task get
fulfilled. I can do the work and deliver
exceptional results. I possess a
combination of skills and experience
that make me stand out.

TRAINING

1998-1999 JOHN R. POWERS (COMMERCIALS)

2006-2008 SOUTHWEST COLLEGE (THEATER)

2015-2016 RMCONAIR RADIO ST. (PODCAST)

ABOUT ME
I love reading and helping others
by giving words of encouragement.
I'm a mother with one son whose
the light of my life. My goal is to
become self sufficient putting
myself in position to open doors
for others. I'm very energetic, free
spirit and ambitious. I host my
own live TV show " Global Street
Wave " offering interviews and
speaking on real life topics.

WWW.FACESOFRAPMOTHERS.COM

The rappers have gone in and created a lot of hit music based upon my influence. And they'll tell you if you ask. -Issac Hayes

WWW.FACESOFRAPMOTHERS.COM

HAVE AN INFLUENCE
A POSITIVE ONE

CHAPTER SIX

ANGELA GILCHRIST-GUYTON

ANGELA GILCHRIST-GUYTON

Hello lovelies, I have been ecstatic with the birth of my new baby girl (grandbaby) Leighani, now over a year old. I am blessed, yet again, to be tickled pink. Leighani warms my heart with so much joy. It's amazing to be a mother and a grandmother. I love each one of my very amazing and talented now grown-up kids; but it's a vastly different kind of love for your grandbabies. You have to experience it for yourself; it is indescribable. She looks like me, with my eyes, and it's almost scary how much she looks like my daughter's and my baby pics. It's as if I've been born three times, lol.

In August of 2019, I had the honor to travel to Atlanta Georgia to meet with OgDuv MacDpg. I signed under TEAM FAULT LINE RECORD label. Duv Mac is an original member of DOGG POUND. I recorded a new single with Duv Mac titled, "Coming for Your Love."

I'm officially going by the name *PurJa' The Queen of The Katt Pound,* now; the release is available on YouTube currently, "if" you would like to hear it. I appreciate the support. While on YouTube, don't forget to "LIKE" and "SUBSCRIBE" to our channel. Make certain you hit the bell to be notified when new music videos are posted.

Your help with ratings means a lot . . .
WINK WINK Kiss Kiss ! ! !

The title on YouTube is, *Coming for Your Love FT PurJa' the Queen of the Katt Pound.*

While in Atlanta, I also had an opportunity to meet with my son, Guy Mitchell. He also signed with the record label: *OgDuv MacDpg Team Fault Line Records.* While recording, *Coming for Your Love,* my son Guy and Duv Mac wrote and rapped together.

I was able to sing the hook for the song they were working on, which released early 2020!

More good news . . . soon, you'll be hearing from my daughter Nya, also signed under Duv Mac's label.

As you can see, I am a quintessential "Rap Mother."

At this time, we are remarkably busy writing new songs and extremely excited to record, release, and perform in the near future. We have felt a little impact from COVID-19 but are working to overcome it!

Additionally, this year *Faces of Rap Mothers*, which I'm featured in, was released. *Faces of Rap Mothers* is a contemporary compilation of beautiful, extraordinary, and phenomenally strong woman who have backgrounds and personal experiences within and among the rap and hip-hop music industry. It is a great book.

If you want to obtain a copy of, *Faces of Rap Mothers* visit the website at www.facesofrapmothers.com or at the publisher's website www.donnaink.net or visit fine book retailers, such as AMAZON and Barnes & Noble.

Thank you for being great supporters – I am so grateful to each of you!

Love Always Angel Gilchrist-Guyton better known as
PurJa' The Queen of the Katt Pound.

"Songs are for ears but melody with lyrics which touch your heart is for your soul."

Furio the Rap Mother

COMING
FOR YOUR LOVE

Love sees no gender #LoveisLove
www.facesofrapmothers.com

Stay Beautiful
and Blooming

WWW.FACESOFRAPMOTHERS.COM

CHAPTER SEVEN

TIFFANI
LEWIS

Tiffani Lewis

Tiffani Lewis, with her empowering lyrics and strong, has a soulful voice that is impacting the music scene and creating a buzz. This 31-year-old songstress from California, is a driving force for women's empowerment, setting her own standard with an attitude that can't be compromised.

Born July 27th in Arizona, Tiffani moved to Pomona shortly after. She has called Pomona home ever since. Some of her earliest, and fondest, memories are of her singing with her Grandmother. Every day, the two practiced in the living room for hours. Not before long, Tiffani developed her own passion for singing and undeniable talent, which became evident to everyone she encountered.

In the winter of 1991, at the age of 4, Tiffani made her first solo debut singing in a Christmas play at her church. This performance was the first of many to come as she remains an active parish member today. It was there, on that platform, she realized singing was her life's ambition.

One day in Junior High after hearing Tiffani's voice during practice, her drama teacher encouraged her to try out for the choir. She was accepted upon completing the audition and continued to sing with this choir through the end of High School. Currently, she has joined forces with *Havoc the Mouthpiece*, from the legendary group *South Central Cartel*. In doing so, she came aboard the entire *GaimChng3r & Go Hard* movement, landing a spot in a group known as the *Magnificent 7*.

This specific arrangement of artists was handpicked by Havoc himself with one goal in mind - greatness. The mix of their creative differences, and lyrical talents, have come together to create an entirely a new sound and achieved just that. This in turn, led to her new Hit Single "#Pain." Written by Chanel Royale and Cali Pitts and produced by Cary Calvin and Robert Baney, "#Pain" embodies an emotion many women can relate to. Inspired by actual events, the tangible feeling and depth of the song is undeniable.

Continuously pushing through barriers and charting new waters, this R&B Diva is the acclaimed New Princess of the West Coast and will not stop until the world knows it too.

RAP ARTIST
TIFFANI LEWIS.

51

GAMECHANGERS

Tiffani Lewis

*RapMother

RAP MOTHER TIFFANI LEWIS

CHAPTER EIGHT

ROLANDA SHEMWELL
GREER MACHARIA

I was born in 1970 to Roland Shoulders and Patricia Bothuel in Detroit Michigan where the Motown Sound was alive and well! As far back as I can remember, I loved to sing and write songs and poetry. My mom and dad both had beautiful voices. Mom used to sing soprano songs such as, *My Guy* and *Wait A Minute Mr. Postman* while dad sang blues, *Dust by Broom* or *Down-Home Blues*! Music was part of who I was. I really enjoyed it.

I was raised in Los Angeles California and moved to Hollywood at 14 years of age. During my time in California, I met and married Craig Even Shemwell. Craig was the son of a popular entertainer, Sylvia Shemwell. She was the lead singer for the group, *The Sweet Inspirations* who traveled with Elvis Presley until he died. They continued touring afterward and took their annual performance around the world and to Graceland (Elvis's estate).

The group included the late Whitney Houston's mother Cissy Houston. They were background singers for Elvis Presley, Aretha Franklin, and many more. Sylvia made her own records too, such as: *Hot Butterfly*. What a voice! Our house was always the house everyone wanted to visit because once we all got together, we would sing, and it turned into an all-night concert. Not to mention, Craig and I entertained with dominos and spades ~ typical husband and wife shenanigans. We had some great times!

I remember meeting Charlie Wilson from the *Gap Band*, Ike Turner, and Whitney Houston for the 1st time. Everyone was down to earth. Nippy (Whitney's nickname) was a delight. Her brother Mike Houston was always nice, and also down to earth.

Craig and I had four children during our marriage: La'Shadion, Cornische, Ashley, and Sara. After we divorced, I later remarried and had another daughter, Deja with husband Michael. My kids are special to me; I love the fact each of them is uniquely carving their own path.

La'Shadion is an entrepreneur, singer, barber by trade, and city councilman. He's also an advocate for injustice and a great dad!

My son Cornische started businesses helping promote the theme of not waiting for someone to give you a job when you can own your own.

My daughter Ashley is headed to law school. By age 26, she had bought three homes. She's a financial go-getter - one who puts her financial goals into perspective and executes them.

My daughters Sara, Deja, and Ashley all love music! Sara has two beautiful daughters, who she loves to sing to! Deja has made four music videos.

I'm always cheering my children on!

Today, my life is incredibly awesome! Twenty-one years ago, I accepted Christ as my Lord and Savior. Now, I teach the younger kids to know God loves us. I attend an amazing Apostolic and Prophetic Church, *F.G.F.D.T. Church*. Pastor Apostle Gemma Valentine has established and taught us to look outside of the four walls of the church AND be the church.

I'm a youth teacher, on the praise team. I minister God's word. I own a nonprofit organization called L.I.F.T. R&R. We help provide resources and referrals to people in need. I truly have had life changing events; all of them built my faith and caused me to . . . *look to the hills which cometh my help*. My help comes from the Lord! God has supplied us with great resources ourselves, such as our supporting partner *Aleph 2 Omega* and its founder James Moss Sr., who has been instrumental in helping L.I.F.T.R&R achieve goals.

As Director over our audio-visual department, running his own *Aleph 2 Omega* FB, YouTube, and website, James has opened a platform where God is glorified. People can use their ministry gifts from all over the world to help others with spiritual growth. The body of Christ can fellowship one with another regardless of where they are attending church.

I am grateful for my life and all the amazing blessings God has bestowed upon me! My husband James Macharia, my five children, my seventeen grandchildren, my love for music, my salvation and so much more remain amazing blessings.

The reason I tell you this is that as a young fifteen-year-old, the family I married into exposed me to cocaine – they used recreational drugs often. I didn't know what it was. Living with Craig, I was offered the first drug in my life with his family at age fifteen. Additionally, I was beaten by Craig and remained afraid. I felt like I had nowhere to turn to and no place else to go. At age sixteen, I was arrested for possession of narcotics. I found I was pregnant with my first son, La'Shadion at that time. I secured subsidized housing so when my baby was born, March 1987, I had a home to bring him to.

Although I was depressed, and on drugs, and being abused by my child's father . . . I remained in my marriage because I didn't know where else to go or what else to do. At age seventeen, I was arrested again for sales of narcotics. This time they threatened to take my La'Shadion from me. He was nearly two years of age at the time. I decided I had to find a better life in order to be a good mom; so, I stopped using drugs and went to Rosston Security college to study and become a security guard.

Not having gotten a high school diploma made job opportunities difficult. Security Guard work paid $7.00 per hour and at the time that wasn't bad. I had no money and needed to provide for my child and, now, had another on the way.

By 1990, I'd finished school with two children, had two jobs and worked as a Security Guard by day for Bank of America and as a waitress in the evening at *Chef's Take Out* in Van Nuys. I came home one day after work to find Ike Turner (Tina Turner's ex-husband) in our home with my husband Craig. His mother Sylvia and several others were smoking crack around my toddler and infant son. So that Craig didn't snap and hurt me, I held my composure, even though I was infuriated. Instead, I asked Craig to let me go to Detroit for a two-week vacation to visit my mother. He answered, "Yes."

His mother gave me $500.00 and bought a greyhound bus ticket to Detroit. I took our children and left and took money I had in the bank along with the $500.00 to secure an apartment. I also looked for jobs and even applied at McDonalds. After three interviews I still didn't land the job with them. With no High School diploma and two children and zero income in a city with limited employment opportunities – I was between a rock and a hard place. I lived in East Side Detroit, a very poverty-stricken neighborhood. Eventually, I applied for welfare and received $26.00 per month. Welfare paid gas and rent directly, and I was given the difference. In my case, this was $26.00. When I notified the government, my check was only $26.00 and not enough to buy pampers, I was told pampers are a luxury, not a necessity.

I immediately realized my chances at securing a decent life for us were better back in California, not in Detroit. However, I remained in Detroit until February 1991. After nearly a year of trying to manage alone, I called my husband Craig to ask if the children and I could come home. Craig bought plane tickets for us; when I arrived in Los Angeles, my husband still was using drugs and having relationships with other women just as before. I had left, so it wasn't surprising.

I knew I still had to fight for a better life for my children. I enrolled in Antelope Valley College's GED program and . . . while earning my GED, I was pregnant with our third daughter. After getting my GED - I immediately enrolled in another college to become a medical assistant.

I graduated!

During my internship, I was offered a job with the Holman Group in Canoga Park as their Medical Insurance Verification

Specialist. After taking the job, I moved my family into a home in Pacoima. At that time, I also applied as a Los Angeles Police Officer. I passed a written and oral exam. The background check had begun, this is where neighbors are interviewed, etc. It was looking good but then another time I came home from work and Craig and his friends were smoking crack in our home. I put everyone out and made my mind up to go to court to file a temporary restraining order to get Craig out the house. I did it – the court gave me a temporary restraining order, but before he was served, he fought with me. He cut my clothes and threw them in the front yard. I got a knife to cut his clothes and then realized I had bought them and didn't want to waste the money by destroying them. Craig stood in front of me and blocked the door to our home; he wouldn't let me enter the house and promised to elbow me if I tried to come in. I continued to walk past him - his back was to me. He turned to elbow me and consequently his side went into the blade I was holding. When I saw the blood on his shirt, I immediately dialed 911 immediately advising them of what happened.

My husband was taken to the hospital. I was taken into custody. I remained in custody for two to three days as detectives interviewed and sorted out what occurred. I was released. All charges were dismissed. At that time, Craig and I separated. LAPD informed me since I had come into contact with the police, even though charges were dropped, I was not allowed to reapply for the LAPD for five years into the future. There went my dream of being a peace officer.

Craig and I reconciled afterward. We had a fourth daughter, Sara in September 1995. I was made aware my husband was having an affair with another lady who claimed to be having his child. It was the final straw and resulted in final dissolution of our marriage because I filed for divorce. After that, we never got back together.

In 1998, I met Michael Greer, we had a daughter, Deja and were married. In February of 1999, Michael was drunk driving, involved in a failure to yield with police. He was sentenced to four years in prison. Then, I had five children, and my husband was incarcerated, but I continued to work and progress.

In 2000, my ex-husband Craig, lay in bed with his fiancé when his best friend came and summoned him outside. The friend shot him dead in the chest. They'd had an argument earlier in the day. By the time I arrived at Holy Cross Medical Center in North Hollywood, my sister and I were informed Craig was dead on arrival. He'd been shot in the chest and the bullet pierced his lungs. He suffocated. I was riddled with pain and regret. I wondered if I had stayed with him, would he be deceased? I had to pull myself together for the sake of my kids and continue to strive for a better future for us all.

After his release from prison, my husband Michael and I moved to McKinney Texas in 2005. Four of my five children graduated from high school there, three at McKinney North and one at McKinney Boyd. My youngest graduated in 2016 and the oldest in California.

I've worked at the same company, formerly known as Countrywide Home Loans, now Bank of America, since November 2001 until current time.

On 22 October 2015, my husband died in our home at 1016 Scenic Hills Drive, McKinney, Texas 75071, due to a house fire. After our home caught fire, I was asked to speak as a victim for the Red Cross and discuss how the Red Cross assisted us as a family in a time of crisis. I delivered a good speech. After speaking, I was asked to join the disaster assistance team and become hands on helping others. I did. I also begin co-chairing

McKinney National's *Back to Church* initiative. In September each year, we put together a no charge rally to invite all City of McKinney residents to church. We invited other churches to come together and provide representation - so if people in McKinney were looking for a place to worship - they had people to speak with face-to-face in order to ask questions and get answers in real-time.

As an active member of *Eternity Community Church,* I sing on our praise and worship team; I also teach Sunday School and serve as the Announcement Clerk. For the past ten years living in Texas, I've continued working with our church. In November of 2001, I was hired with Home Loans as management, then I was promoted to their workforce management team and able to work from home for Bank of America.

In total, I purchased three homes, the first in Rosamond California; we then built our home in McKinney Texas, which burned down. After that, I purchased another home in Anna Texas. It was my dream to be the first person in our family to break a cycle of poverty and be a homeowner. I have achieved my dream. Buying and owning a home wasn't discussed in our family before that time. I wanted to provide stability for my children, giving them someone to look up to and something they could feel proud of.

Today, my daughter Ashley at twenty-two years of age is in college and has purchased her first home with her husband. I am happy to be able to say I succeeded in teaching my children.

The Incident of the Dog Bite

My husband, while we were McKinney Texas, had two dogs. One was a pregnant female, the other a male. These dogs were rescued during the fire. When I received the news, my husband died in the fire, I was informed his dogs were saved. The next month of my life was filled with planning a memorial service for my husband and getting his family from Nevada, Arizona, and

California here, while living temporarily with my son when I could no longer live in the hotel I stayed in as our home was destroyed.

My two-week bereavement was over. Since I worked from home with a bank issued laptop, I was required to have private WiFi instead of public and the hotel was no longer an option for me. The female dog had given birth to her puppies and I had to have a place for a dog and puppies and a kennel wasn't going to take them.

In November of 2015, I was living at my son's home. The dog with puppies was in a kennel in our home and was let outside into the backyard. The puppies and kennel were at the top of the stairs. Sometime after 11am, I heard a knock at the front door and went to open it. I found a few people standing there asking if it was my dog on the back porch. I explained I had two dogs but didn't know which one may be on the porch at the time. One of the people at the door was a peace officer. The officer explained the dogs had gotten out of the yard. One was shot and killed. The other shot but they believed the dog ran back into the yard and up the stairs. Apparently, she was shot in the chest, so they didn't know what condition she was in.

I allowed the officer, and animal control worker with her, to walk with me through my son's room to where the back door was located. When I opened the door, our female dog was bleeding and laying on the top the stairs next to her kennel where her pups were. She was breathing heavily. I began crying. It was too much for me to take in in less than a month.

My home and all I owned was demolished. My husband of nineteen years had died. Our daughter was a mess mentally having lost her father as his only child. Now, his dogs were killed by police. I had a memorial for my husband less than two weeks earlier and was already back at work with two-week bereavement being over. I was now homeless, needing a permanent home for our daughter and me. It was complete mental overload – I was overwhelmed.

The lady officer told me she was going to go to the hospital to talk with the injured woman and would get back to me. At this time, I called work letting them know I had to sign off for the day. I told my boss what happened, then called my mother at work. She heard me crying hysterically and left work to come check on me. My oldest son also came home after my mother called him and told him the condition, I was in. Prior to either of them arriving, there was another knock at the door. This time it was animal control advising me our dog was not doing well and having a hard time breathing. She advised they could release our dog to me for immediate surgery at a veterinarian with no guarantee she would make it, "or" I could permit animal control to take her.

The decision was difficult. I cried more and the animal control worker stood with me on the porch and looked into the field across the street. I saw the dog laying on the ground, and she wasn't moving. About three people stood around her. I asked if it was my dog. Animal control said, "Yes." I asked, "She's not moving?" She responded, "Yes, I know, she's not doing well." At that point I signed over my husband's dog to animal control and went inside the house in shock and stunned over all that happened in just thirty days.

Afterward, I didn't hear from the peace officer again. There wasn't a police report with a name of the person who had been injured. A couple weeks later, I was at Walmart in McKinney near Red Bud and University Drive and recognized the police officer shopping. I stopped her to ask about the injured woman and how she was doing. She stated she wasn't able to follow-up with me and she told me to request a copy of the police report.

In December 2015, I received a letter in the mail, which included two tickets with fines for an animal-at-large from the McKinney City Courthouse. I called to confirm it was for one dog and they answered, "There was a fine for each dog." I owed two fines and had to pay by a specific date or come to court on a certain date. I paid nearly $600.00. I asked if that was all that was required and the court clerk said, "Yes." I heard nothing about the incident again in the future.

Later, I bought a new home in Anna Texas and moved there with my daughter on 16 January 2015. We then went on a much-needed vacation June of 2016. When we returned to the United States, I was arrested at the airport in front of my daughter. I wasn't told why I was being detained until an hour later after my escort from the airplane to customs detention. At that time, I was told I had a $20,000.00 warrant from Collin County for a dog bite with serious bodily injury.

At that time, I was taken to Houston County jail and remained there for two days until a $2,900.00 bond was posted. After achieving the bond, I was back in Anna Texas and informed by Collin County Sheriff's Department I needed to come in to be booked within ten days of my release from the Houston Jail. So, the next day (Tuesday), after work, I went to the jail and processed in. Thankfully, they released me since I was already on bond. It was unbelievable.

MY SPIRITUAL TESTIMONY

Before accepting Christ, I began having dreams nightly that it was the end of the world. In these dreams, people were running to escape fire raining from the sky and major earthquakes where the ground opened and swallowed them alive. There were tsunamis. In each of these dreams, I didn't repent. Instead, I asked God to save my children. I didn't feel worthy of salvation. I was depressed, I even considered suicide. I had lost all hope in the goodness of people. This began as a teen from an abusive and broken homelife where I'd become homeless and had to sleep on bus benches or in abandoned hotels. I was addicted to drugs for a while too. On one occasion, I wanted to commit suicide, the only thing that kept me holding was my children.

In thinking about moving to my sisters' homes in earlier years, I knew I had children and couldn't put more kids on either of them. Instead, I called a friend, the cousin of my new husband, who was a devout Christian and showed it through love of others. I told him how I felt. He told me he would take me and the children to church. He did. I was introduced to six women who studied the Bible with me for another six months before I accepted Christ as my personal savior.

Honestly, still, at the time, I felt there were deep reasons God wouldn't accept me into his kingdom.

What did you hear?

Finally, after the Spirit of God and people in my life continued to tell me God loves me and sent his son to die for me and my soul was precious to him, I became baptized. The scripture that inspired me is from Jeremiah 29:11.

> *"For I know the plans I have for you declares the Lord, plans to prosper you and not to harm you, plans to give you hope and a future".*

I knew then God had always loved and protected me. I remembered the dreams recollecting how he showed me the destruction surrounding my life. He loved me enough to warn me and draw me closer to him. I realized he was there all the time. I am saved for sixteen years now.

Today, I have dedicated my life to the work of the ministry and attend church regularly to learn more of God and how to be a servant for him to reach the lost. I work with our church's outreach program. We go to the streets and door-to-door to tell the good news of the Gospel.

Of my five children, I have eleven grandchildren and seventeen great-grandchildren. I have been blessed by Christ and my spirit is filled with joy.

ROLANDA MACHARIA

WWW.FACESOFRAPMOTHERS.COM

Note to self:

Don't let bad days keep you down. Keep a childlike spring in your step and, when in doubt, have a good pillow fight!

CHAPTER NINE

FEDRA THOMPSON

Fedra Thompson!

TO EVERYONE'S IDOL,

RAP
MOTHERS
SAVE
THE DAY

YOU'RE THE BEST!

FEDRA AND FRIENDS

RAP MOTHER

www.facesofrapmothers.com

CHAPTER TEN

JAMIKA SMITH
LOVE WISDOM

Kingdom Blessing Faces of Rap Mother's and Family!!
Give Thanks in Everything, For God Loves You!

As I set here soul searching, reflecting on this past year's victories and shortcomings, I can't help but feel gratitude about what this year has unveiled. I think about how some of us have lost love ones while others gained new additions to our family. Doors of opportunity have opened for some and doors for transitioned closed for others. *Ecclesiastes 3:1* states:

> *"To everything there is a season, and a time to every purpose under the heaven."*

In everything, we must find a reason to be thankful for time and memories shared with souls who have transitioned to the next life. We are able to receive blessings through learned lessons and the smiles, ups, and downs we've shared. And, we are able to realize if God allowed our love ones to stay here on earth just for our own selfish reasons, it may hold up the process of the circle of life.

God has a plan and reason He allows things to happen. He promises us to give us beauty for our ashes. I have remarkably close friends who lost sons this year. It was such a trying time for them because the guys left children behind. One friend's daughter was eight months pregnant when she had to say goodbye to her husband. I mourned for them with many tears and hurt knowing there is a void where there was once fulfillment.

But once the first grandson was born, so much joy overshadowed their hearts and made the void not so empty anymore. I smiled so hard and thought to myself. why Lord, your word doesn't lie!

He said in the *Book of Isaiah 61:3*:

> *"To appoint unto them that mourn in Zion, to give unto them beauty for ashes, the oil of joy for mourning, the garment of praise for the spirit of heaviness; that they might be called trees of righteousness, the planting of the Lord, that he might be glorified".*

What an awesome Father God he is who does things, so our sadness or shortcomings have an expiration date! It is all in the way we choose to deal with a thing. If we continue to trust, He loves us and always has our best interest in mind. We are rewarded for not giving up on His faithfulness he has toward us. His children love and trust Him.

So, as we move through the year, let's put on the *Spirit of Gratefulness and Give Thanks to the Lord and our Savior Jesus Christ* for loving us. He gave His life for us to live in liberation from circumstances that keep us in bondage and despair. We are children of the Most High God and have a promise He will never leave us or forsake us, even to the ends of the earth . . . Amen!

If you wish to contact me, I can be contacted through Facebook "Jamika Loves Wisdom" or Al And Jazz "LifeChangers" Ministry or through email: alanjazzministries@gmail.com

*And remember that it's always . . .

"Love because God is Love ~Be Blessed"

CHAPTER ELEVEN

SHARON LYNETTE YOUNG

SHARON LYNETTE-YOUNG

I'm sitting here thinking about when I first met Candy Strother DeVore Mitchell. We both lived in Hollywood on different sides of the city. I happened to be near where Candy lived, at McDonalds with my children on a day they wanted McDonalds – while eating we met Candy.

Aurelia was about five years old; Ricky was about two, and Indica was about one month old. We were sitting there eating when this young lady walked up to me. She was very nice and all over me lol. She thought I looked so much like Janet Jackson she had to come and talk to me. This was October 1986; I had just moved back to California having just had Indica.

So, we started talking. She asked for my number because she wanted to take me by the Dabarge house to meet James Dabarge because he was married to Janet. She wanted to see his reaction to me, she thought I looked so much like Janet Jackson. She also told me her and James were dating so it was cool we change numbers. She did make that happen. We met up and went to their place. They lived in Burbank at the time.

We would do a lot of hanging out after that. We were at all kids at events like *Beverly Hills Cop* movie premieres, *Golden Child* after parties, and much more. We ran the streets of Hollywood and met all kinds of people. We applied for and got jobs in movies as extras dancing in music videos, etc. Soon after, I started showcasing Aurelia because she really could sing, and she wasn't shy.

Remember, I had two younger children my mom would care for them while we got to hang out in Hollywood and meet different people like Eddie Murphy and many more. Aurelia started sing when she was about two years old. Her favorite song was *Ring My Bell*. She sounded so good at two – at about six years old we are in Hollywood and determined to go hard and see what we could make happen with her career. We set her up with the *Way to Happiness Club*, she was in the recording studio and we met Hank Ross. His son was in the business. He was a child star (actor) Sharvar Ross he was known for his role on different strokes as Dudley. Then, his father helped us met people, getting Aurelia showcased. She worked with some famous actors and actresses, such as, Alfonso Rebarro, Tina Yothers, and Sharvar Ross.

They performed at the *Bob Hope Club* on Ivar Street in Hollywood. My sister Donna, and myself, were background singers for the show. She was so little. Her mom and Aunty sang back up for her. LMAFO! Donna and I couldn't, and still cannot, sing we had to give her backup, so she did so good. They never paid us much attention.

Aurelia was the Little Star. Everybody loved her. She just would get on stage and go for it. No shame. No fear. She killed it every time with standing ovations at every show. She sang cover tunes, such as *The Greatest Love of All* by Whitney Huston. She loved Anita Baker - her favorite song was Anita's. We took her to Hollywood Boulevard on weekends, at Highland and Hollywood Boulevard, at the square where people go to dance, sing, and hang out. Everything was happening there on the weekend. It was the place to be. So, we would take a mike and speaker and put it on a box in front of Aurelia and let her sing.

People came by and put money into her box - not just dollars people put tens and twenties. We did this every Friday and Saturday. She would make about three hundred and fifty dollars. Then on Sunday we would go to Venice Beach and sit out there, and Aurelia would sing her little heart out. People loved her. They would put tens and twenties out of their pockets and purses too. The more money she would see go in the box the more she gave it to them. I mean she sang! Lol.

She reminded me of some friends Crystal Penny and Shanice Wilson. Their mom and aunty would sing behind her when they were little girls, the only different is that their mom and Aunty could sing and had beautiful voices. With us, only Aurelia could sing. We just faked it using background vocals on the song, but it was so new to us and so much fun being young and living in Hollywood.

Speaking of Shanice Wilson, I met her when she was about fourteen years old. She had already done star search and had won the competition. She was about to release her first album, *I Love Your Smile*. She was dating my nephew Michael Owens at the time. She has always had family and close friends supporting her. I love them so much. I also look up to them because they show you what family is supposed to be about.

They love and support one another, being there when you need your family and being there for each other though good and bad times. They don't give up on one another. When time gets tuff – they help each other make it through the hard times. With that level of support, everything else can be a walk in the park. This is what and how I wanted to give thanks to Shanice and her family by letting them know people pay attention to them. I still love how they manage together. I have mad respect for them for doing what they do. I'm forever proud to know them. We shared some great moments together and I will always pray they remain happy and successful.

God shows us what love is supposed to look and feel like. Looking at how Shanice and Flex's relationship is sweet, humble, and caring with respect, love, and understanding. Love is patient with good communication and more. I feel that is what my husband Eric Berry and I have. Nothing and no one can come between us. We were given to one another by the Most High. Our journey together is sealed forever.

So, thank you Flex and Shanice for yawls example of one true love and life.

Let's shift gears to 1997 living in North Hollywood California at 11350 Otsego Street. I had a three-bedroom townhome style apartment with an upstairs and downstairs. It was the first time in a long time it was just me and my children.

I hadn't lived without other family members in an exceptionally long time. I always had my own place; I just would let other family members move in because they would need a place to stay. In 97 we were in our own place and my children were getting older. Ricky was still in Detroit with his dad at the time intending to join us in Cali. He was in school in Detroit. Aurelia was still a budding artist and going to school. Channerik was about nine years old and Indica was about twelve years old going to school. I was braiding hair and trying to figure out what I really wanted to do.

About this time, I met Kimba. She was married to a longtime friend of mine, Alba. I used to do work for him, little jobs here and there. He and his wife Kimba opened a hair Salon and beauty supply shop right around the corner from where I moved to. Kimba would ask me who braided my hair. I told her I breaded it. She was shocked because the braids were so neat. She didn't know it took me about a week to do them myself. One day she said, "You should just come braid for me you don't need a license to braid you are so good at it."

I thought about it. That's when I went and asked her if I could work for her and braid. She said, "Yes." And then I really started to meet all kinds of people. I began doing hair for all types of industry folks, such as Alonzo Roberson from ASCAP publishing, Big Chuck from Interscope Records, Eric B & Rakim, Riza, Shyheim, U-God, Wu-Tang Clan, Old Dirty Bastard, and then met a hair stylist named Dr Boogie who did everyone you want to name's hair. So, I started working with as his assistant and began meeting everybody. The shop got me working with people such as Berry Gordy's grandson, Britney Spear's dancers, walk-in up and coming rap artists or up and coming singing groups, Xzibit, etc.

With Dr Boogie I worked with people such as Debbie Allen, Kim Whitley, Lisa Raye, Rocky from 706 in Park, and Stockholm Syndrome out of Switzerland. All kinds of behind the scene producers and writers of TV shows and movies you see on television and in theaters. I did Tiffney Hashish's hair for the shop and wound-up working backstage with Dr Boogie who did makeup while I did hair getting actors, actresses and musicians ready to hit the stage. It felt so good because they were touring hairstyles, I was doing for them – when it looks good – you feel good. I was a part of something great. No one can take these accomplishments away from me.

Back then I was making a lot of money. I had clients like Sir Jinx. I worked from 7 am until 3 am every day and barely getting any sleep. If someone knocked on my door, I got up out of my sleep to do their hair, that is how dedicated I was to clients. I worked on Handy Moms TV show, Raising Whitley TV show, Real Estate Stories TV show, Theater Awards and with Vivica Foxx on Infomercials. Privately, I braided her hair for four of her movies.

As years go by, doing work like this, you meet more and more people doing what you do. There was a pizza place right next to a shop I worked at called Diamonds. It was the same place I worked when I first started doing hair in a shop. It was called, One Stop. Kimba and Alba owned it then. Now, Diamond owned it years later - about six years later. Working for Diamond, I was getting paid again, after 911 had passed and all the devastation. People were trying to get their lives back in order.

So were the pizza guys. Mario was telling people he was going to sell his restaurant. Diamond was saying her brother was thinking about getting it. This was crazy because my mom and had been trying to find a location for a restaurant for a couple years and the spot next to the shop I worked in would bring business. I knew dam near everyone in the area. We thought this could be really good and I'm one of the best cooks in the world. I knew people would go crazy for real soul food not water down soul fool that makes you take a nap after eating it. I mean soooo good you don't want stop eating.

We had all the comedians coming to the restaurant. Kenny and Kale (Kale) loved the Apple Cobbler. Flex loved the Chili Dogs. Many folks liked the baked chicken glazed with Russian dressing. We brought fried fish to the hood. Lol, including bass, catfish, red snapper, tilapia, whiting, etc. We made Kool-Aide and much more. It was favorite time in life because after all the time in Hollywood, I knew we were about to take off, but it didn't work out.

Instead, I met my husband, Eric Charles Berry, right out in front of the restaurant selling his CDs and movies. He would come in and order a catfish sandwich and large Kool-Aid. He had come to LA for the Soul Train awards. He'd come with a chick he called his cousin Vash aka (Swiss Barbie bone). She left him stranded in the valley. He got my number somehow and called me. I picked him up and let him sleep in my car that night. I don't know why. I felt for his current situation. His family was up North. Vash had locked all his stuff up in her house. His ID, his CD maker, his clothes; basically, everything he owned so he couldn't even buy a ticket to get back up North.

We started hanging out together because I was also homeless at the time. Even though I was working in the restaurant. It way my idea to open it but I didn't have the money to do it, so the family did. They had all the control - so I did my part and left. I wanted something to work in the family where we could do something together to make something big happen and become successful together as a family.

I was going to school for cosmetology and working at Diamonds. It was hard sleeping in the car, sometimes on the roof of my old three-bedroom town house, wishing I were living back in there. I kept moving forward striving to make it happen. Eric and I became closer and closer. We started making planes for our future. He asked me to become his wife. I said, "Yes!" And, we started renting rooms in the Pepper Tree on Lankershim Boulevard, which is the main place we stayed. Another location was on Van Owen and we stayed there for months. We had a refrigerator in our room, our own bathroom, and a kitchen downstairs where we could cook food. It was nice coming off of the street - very appreciated.

Today, we have *Off the Planet Productions* - our recording studio, our business, and our home. At this location we rent studio time at thirty dollars an hour for recording, for sixty dollars an hour and one-hundred dollars and hour for mastering. We have worked with Omar Gooding and his Moe Doe family, Sticky Fingers, Venus Leone (she is a great artist and engineer and loves my chicken), and Pressplayy (he is a very good producer but goes around using and lying to people to use the studio - he can't seem to keep one of his owned studios - he gets put out everywhere he goes).

I'm glad we have a good relationship with our landlord because if not she would have just thrown us out, but God is good. It's sad because if we had really come together we could have done some major things out here but because you have people like Pressplayy trying to get over on everybody . . . he gets pennies and acts like he did it by himself. He's so afraid of sharing, he ends up with nothing. Anyway, if he shared, he would see the whole team would bring something to the table. If we share, we end up better off because we all win.

We keep it pushing forward. We have clients renting out the studio and our *Off the Planet Productions* t-shirt and hat line, *Living in London*, and *Ice Cream Caken'it* and the *Eric Berry and Perish Wallace TV Show* partnered with Wallace Films. Perish and Eric have been friends for an awfully long time, and they were doing Ice Cream Caken'it TV before we even met. Eric works downtown on skid row he does maintenance for S.R.O. Housing and then comes home and starts producing beets and recording clients. He stays busy.

When you have a dream, you have to give your all. No matter how tired you are, you have to keep going. While writing this Chapter, something else that gives me something to be proud of is that since having the first book out – it really feels amazing to be a part of this project with the Faces of Rap Mothers series and "Rap Mothers Save the Day Series" children's books.

My husband, Bobby is incredibly supportive; we work together to get things accomplished. I have a big extended family. We are mostly separated, and I don't know if is due to Hollywood or age, but if we'd worked together with all of the talent, we have there would be no stopping us. I've been really getting into the Bible lately, finding out who I am, where I came from, and what God really wants from me.

So, I am writing a book about how I found I am an Israelite from the tribe of Judah. I'm a descendant of Abraham, Isaac, and Jacob. These forefathers broke the blood covenant with the Most High and our brother and father Yahawah who people call Jesus Christ. This was a big shock to me. At the same time, it makes sense to me. I can relate to something that feels right. So, my way of thinking and eating is changing. I'm getting to know myself all over again. It has been a long journey, and with more to come.

I'm going back to the beginning of this Chapter where I started with Aurelia. We are going to get her LP done with five songs mix mastered and the art for her album. It is all going on social media plate forms with a dope video and will be on all our media outlets. We are going hard, doing shows, we are moving Bobby's TV show forward and *Faces of Rap Mothers – Book One* and *Book Two* plus *Rap Mothers Save the Day – Book One* and *Book Two* will all be released by Thanksgiving 2020. For the children's books, I work up some of the artwork for Candy. Our TV Shows, clothing lines and much more are continuously moving forward.

So, you all will be hearing from us with another book - I won't give much more away – but my own tell all book will be coming soon and feature the good, the bad and the ugly.

In the meantime, if you need to get your songs mastered – you'll appreciate our work – it will be a worthwhile investment so get with us and share!

Design Protection
Certificate

Design combo:
Limited Edition code: #IV83
Shoe name: Rap

Rap Mom Shoes

WWW.FACESOFRAPMOTHERS.COM

SALE
SALE
SALE
SALE

RAP MOTHER'S 5
By Sharon Young (US)
MADE IN ITALY

BROWSE ALL COLLECTIONS

Exaltation involves family & love?

FACES OF RAP MOTHERS

PROGRAMMING

ABOUT THE AUTHOR

CANDY STROTHER
DEVORE MITCHELL

Candy is an actress, author, mom, and executive producer of *The Face of Rap Mothers Show*, which, like her two-book series, is comprised of rap and hip-hop mothers, sisters, aunts, cousins, etc. working to build better futures through entrepreneurial and solo-preneur efforts. She is also CEO of *Black Cash Records* and two of her children are rap and hip-hop artists, namely HONEY and KING THA RAPPER.

Currently, Candy resides in Los Angeles with her children and husband. Her next children's book releases October 2020. Among the Rap Mothers, additional eMagazines and sundry publications are established on a routine basis; however, these are *Faces of Rap Mothers ancillary projects through third-party associations*, and not a part of either book series- there are media rights crossovers, which the parties view as oversights. After getting your hands on this volume - - - check back often to see what the Rap Mothers are up to . . .

ABOUT THE GHOSTWRITER

MS. DONNA LEE QUESINBERRY

Donna L. Quesinberry—known as "Q" to friends, colleagues, and creatives—has been crafting content since she was twelve. Her first client? Her father. He handed her a real estate ad assignment in junior high, and though she hesitated, he said, "Call the Washington Post. Their rep will walk you through it. You're a great writer." He was right. She made the call, wrote the copy, and those ads sold homes for years to come.

Fast-forward to 2026: Q has authored over 473 stories, ghostwritten for countless clients (credited and uncredited), and published more than 25,000 documents across 100+ disciplines for over 200 national and international entities. Her five syndicated columns and New Age Philosophies for Writing Enhancement course reached millions—blending subliminal messaging and neurolinguistics before the field had a name. As the former National Writing Examiner, she built a loyal following pre- and post-social media, always ahead of the curve.

Q's political neutrality is legendary. With deep PAC and junior lobbyist reach-back, she's written for both Republican and Democratic initiatives—without ever revealing her own stance. That kind of discretion is rare, especially in high-stakes environments.

Academically, Q holds over 250 higher learning credits with a GPA north of 3.8. She earned a Certificate in International Affairs focused on Eastern Europe and the Middle East during the Gulf War Crisis, a Technical Writing Certification, and studied Court and Conference Reporting—clocking 225 wpm as a stenographer before pivoting majors due to accreditation loss. She earned dual Bachelor of Science accreditation in Business Administration and Computer Sciences from Strayer University, back when the campus moved weekly across D.C. and she chased it down and was formerly called Strayer College.

Q is the Founder and President of DonnaInk Publications, L.L.C., a small, woman-owned traditional and indie publishing house featuring over 30 authors and their eclectic works for discriminating readers. She's also the dpInk Ltd. Liability Company solopreneur, a boutique management consultancy offering holistic, award-winning approaches to business development, strategic communications, publishing, training, and media management. Her work blends spiritual intention with market precision—delivering results across government and commercial sectors.

At home, Q is Grand'Mere to eleven grandchildren and mother to five successful children. She shared a Historic Registry J.F. Cole Airbnb in Carthage, North Carolina with her adult son, a TBI survivor, and their beloved pets: three cats (Cali, Garfield, Lucius) and two long-haired chihuahuas (Scuddle and Charlotte) – they now reside in Southern Maryland and await the sale of the J. F. Cole Historic Home.

Q remains available for talk radio, televised programming, and speaking engagements. Her ghostwriting and publishing services are active and thriving. She prefers email inquiries at donnaink@gmail.com to regulate her schedule and discourages Facebook messages unless they're for email coordination.

Easygoing, spiritually grounded, and creatively fierce, Q brings top-tier excellence to every discipline she touches. Her legacy is built on trust, talent, and timeless delivery—recognized by long-standing clients, industry peers, and a global readership..

CANDY STROTHER DEVORE MITCHELL

EXTRO

GHOSTWRITING
AND PUBLISHER REQUESTS

A little-known fact, nearly every novice author's original book release results in a host of family and friends reaching out to their publisher requesting representation. **DonnaInk** developed the new author's release rule … anyone reaching out to the publishing house after their friend or relative publishes their first or second book … must wait at least eight (8) months until their submission or ghostwriting ideas can be considered for representation. Writing a book takes discipline. **DonnaInk Publications, L.L.C.** does not accept every book presented to us – we are not vanity or subsidy publishers – we follow traditional and some Indie standards. While the industry has changed, many changes are what the doctor ordered, while others – like overnight work are not. At **DonnaInk** we prefer quality over quantity of our published works, but we do not frown on anyone else's take on publishing – to each his or her own! 😊 So, if you have a book for informing or entertaining "readers" let us hear from you!

For individuals or organizations interested in publishing a book with a message for readers, or stories readers will love, **DonnaInk Publications, L.L.C.'s** website: www.donnaink.net has a submissions link under our About Us dropdown. This is the best way to be considered for potential publisher's representation.

For ghostwriting, a services tab is also featured under our About Us in the dropdown – look for services. Ms. Quesinberry charges industry-standard retainers and fees for ghostwriting. Each year, there are two gratis ghostwriting proffers to give back to the community; however, normally to have a book ghostwritten costs are involved these are not free endeavors. Ghostwriting takes time and energy followed by review, editorial, proofreading and more time and energy. To learn more and access publisher services visit: www.donnaink.net or write to facesofrapmothersghostwriting@gmail.com.

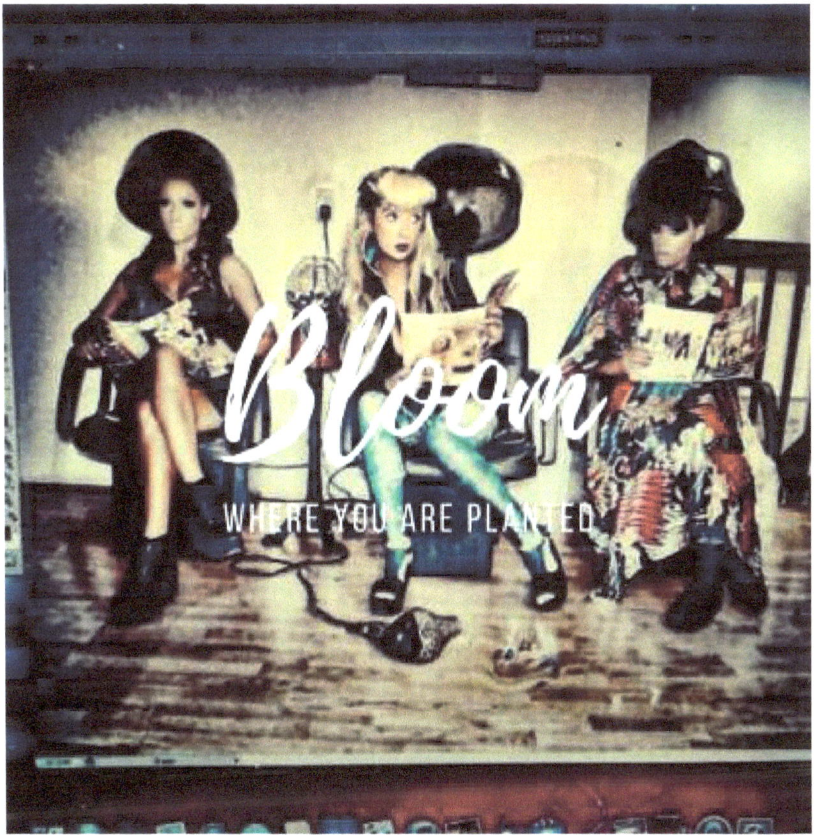
Bloom
WHERE YOU ARE PLANTED

FACES OF RAP MOTHERS
ON SALE NOW
AMAZON

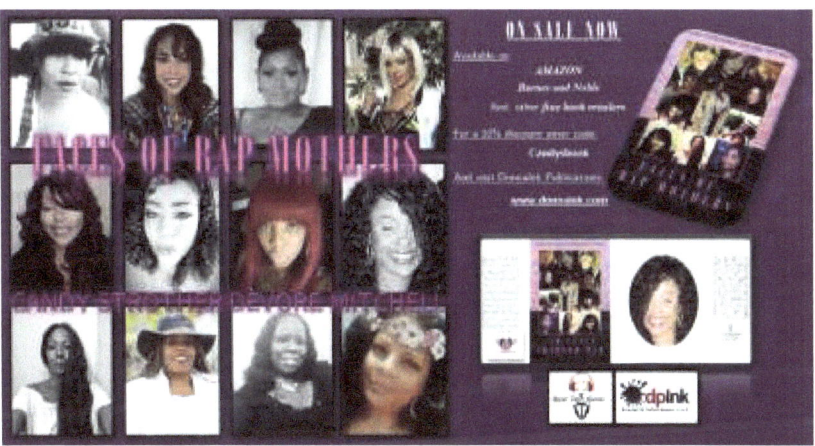

SOCIAL MEDIA

AND
WEBSITES

Rap Mothers Save The Day Children's Series Books!

Faces of Rap Mothers Website

https://www.facesofrapmothers.com

Beat Deep Books | DonnaInk Publications Website

https://www.donnaink.net
(For deep pocket discounts!)

Facebook Fan Page

https://www.facebook.com/facesofrapmothers

Instagram

https://www.instagram.com/facesofrapmothers

Pinterest

https://www.pinterest.com/facesofrapmothers

Twitter

https://www.twitter.com/facesofrapmothers

YouTube

https://www.youtube.com/facesofrapmothers

MERCHANDISE

AND
GIFTS

www.facesofrapmothers.com

Gimme My

Beat Deep Books
DonnaInk Publications, L.L.C.
17611 Aquasco Road
Brandywine, MD 20613
or
1390 Chain Bridge Road, #10029
McLean, VA 22101

www.donnaink.net | www.donnalquesinberry.com
Write to: donnaink@gmail.com

www.ingramcontent.com/pod-product-compliance
Lightning Source LLC
Chambersburg PA
CBHW041411010726
47507CB00005B/241